A Random House PICTUREBACK® Shape Book

Free Puppies
(to Loving Homes)

By Annie Ingle

Illustrated by Bobbi Barto

Random House 🏠 New York

Manufactured in the United States of America 10 9 8 7 6 5 4 3 2

Maggie, the dog next door, had just had puppies. Samantha was so excited!

"May I go see the new puppies now?" she asked her mother.

"Not yet," her mother said. "Not until they're a bit bigger."

Why was Samantha so excited? Because she was going to pick out a puppy of her very own!

"Owning a puppy is a serious business," said her mother. "It means you have to feed it when it's hungry and walk it several times a day. You have to wash it and brush it and hug it and love it forever. Owning a puppy is a *big* responsibility."

"*My* responsibility," Samantha said solemnly.

While Samantha waited to see the puppies, she made a little puppy bed right next to her bed.

She got a bowl
and a brush

and a ball

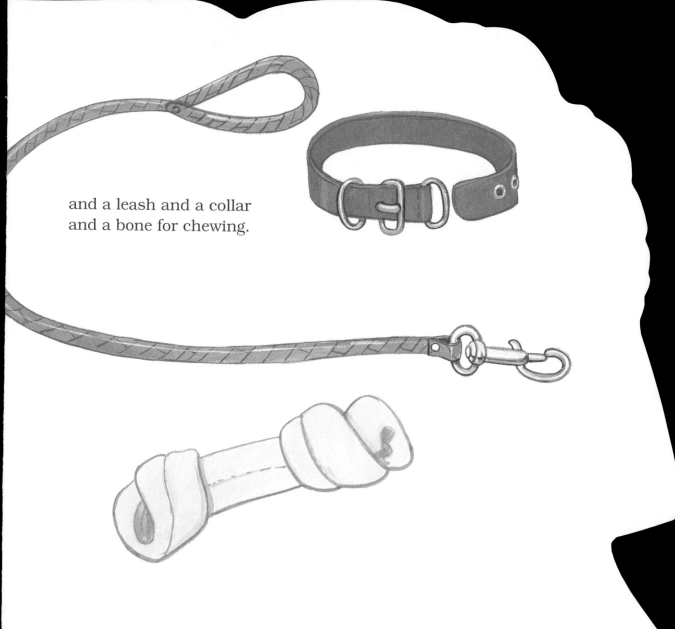

and a leash and a collar
and a bone for chewing.

"Because puppies need to chew things to help their
teeth grow," her mother explained. "Better a bone than
your father's slippers!"

When the puppies were a week old, Samantha was allowed to go next door and see them at last!

They were on the floor of the closet in Mr. McCloskey's study.

Samantha peered in almost shyly. Maggie wagged her tail when she saw Samantha, as if to say, "Aren't my puppies beautiful? Look—but don't touch."

Maggie's puppies squirmed around on her belly and drank milk from her nipples.

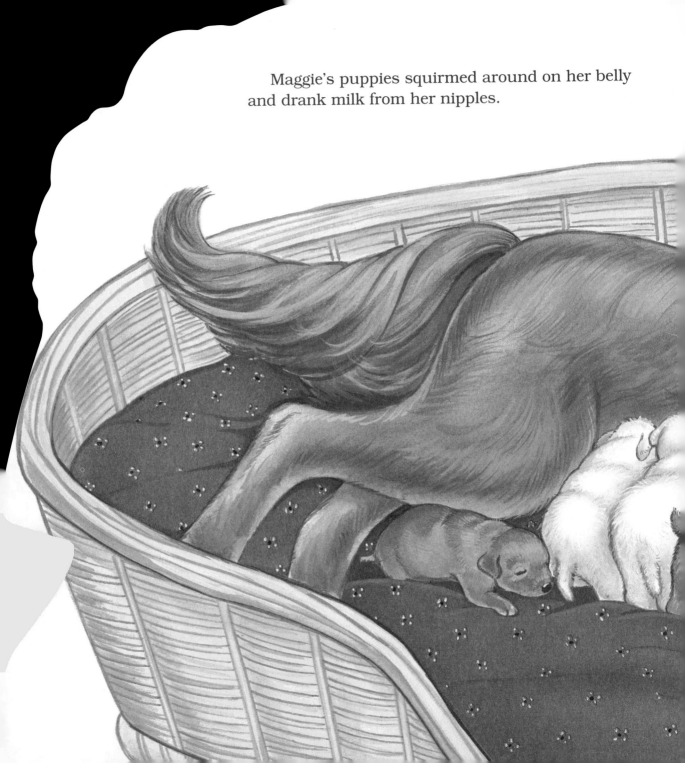

"They're so tiny!" Samantha said breathlessly.
And so cute! Their eyes weren't even open yet.

When Samantha visited five days later, the puppies' eyes were open. But they still squirmed around. "Like fat furry worms!" Samantha said with a giggle.

There were seven of them in the litter. Three were brown and three were white and one—the tiniest of all—was brown and white, with floppy ears. Mr. McCloskey called her the runt.

"*Runt* means the smallest," Samantha told her mother.

The next week, when Samantha went
back to visit, Maggie let her actually hold
the puppies. Samantha knew to be oh so
gentle! They were still tiny enough to fit
in her hands! And they made a noise that
sounded more like a *mew* than a *woof.*
Samantha had never before felt anything
so soft...or so wiggly!

Maggie now let Samantha visit longer. She sat for hours just watching the puppies.

There was one big white one who acted as if he were boss. He kept starting fights. Samantha called him Bossy.

There was a fat white one who was so greedy! He pushed his brothers and sisters away from their mother's nipples. Samantha called him Chubby.

There was one little brown one who liked to chew on Samantha's finger. Samantha called her Scrappy.

And then there was the brown-and-white-speckled runt whose ears were so long she kept tripping over them. Samantha called her Floppy Ears.

One day, when Samantha was saying good-bye to Maggie and her pups, Floppy Ears followed her out of the closet and made a yipping noise that was almost a bark. She seemed to be saying, "Hurry back to see us!"

When the puppies were six weeks old, Mr. McCloskey put up
a sign in his front yard. The sign said FREE PUPPIES (TO LOVING HOMES).

Samantha was first in line.

"I'll take Floppy Ears," she said.

Mr. McCloskey knew just which puppy Samantha meant!

Samantha took Floppy Ears
home to see her bed

and her bowl,

her ball
and her brush
and her bone...

...and gave her a great big "welcome home" hug!